THE CASE OF THE
Wooden
Timekeeper

ERIC HOGAN & TARA HUNGERFORD

FIREFLY BOOKS

FOR WILFRED, PARIS
& THEIR AUNTIES AND UNCLES.

A Firefly Book

Published Under License by Firefly Books Ltd. 2019
Copyright © 2019 Gumboot Kids Media Inc.
Book adaptation and realization © 2019 Firefly Books Ltd.
Photographs © Gumboot Kids Media Inc. unless otherwise
specified on page 32.

This book is based on the popular children's shows *Scout &*
the Gumboot Kids, *Daisy & the Gumboot Kids* and *Jessie & the*
Gumboot Kids.

First printing

Library of Congress Control Number: 2019930776

Library and Archives Canada Cataloguing in Publication:
Title: The case of the wooden timekeeper / Eric Hogan & Tara
Hungerford.
Other titles: Scout & the Gumboot Kids (Television program)
Names: Hogan, Eric, 1979- author. | Hungerford, Tara, 1975-
author. | Imagine Create Media, issuing body.
Description: Series statement: A Gumboot Kids nature mystery |
Based on the TV series: Scout & the Gumboot Kids.
Identifiers: Canadiana 20190058293 | ISBN 9780228101956
(hardcover) | ISBN 9780228101963 (softcover)
Subjects: LCSH: Tree-rings—Juvenile literature. | LCSH: Trees—
Growth—Juvenile literature.
Classification: LCC QK477.2.A6 H64 2019 | DDC j582.16/39—dc23

Published in the United States by
Firefly Books (U.S.) Inc.
P.O. Box 1338, Ellicott Station
Buffalo, New York 14205

Published in Canada by
Firefly Books Ltd.
50 Staples Avenue, Unit 1
Richmond Hill, Ontario L4B 0A7

Printed in Canada

Canada We acknowledge the financial support of the
Government of Canada.

It's a crisp fall afternoon in Dandelion Town.

Scout is stacking firewood, getting ready for the winter. He loves to sit cozy by the fire during chilly evenings.

Here comes Daisy up the path.

"Hello, Daisy" says Scout.

"Hi, Scout! I found a beautiful pinecone that had fallen from a tree. I used it to make a nature craft for you. It's a mini Scout."

"Cool! Thanks, Daisy. Pinecones are awesome, but a pinecone twin is even more awesome!"

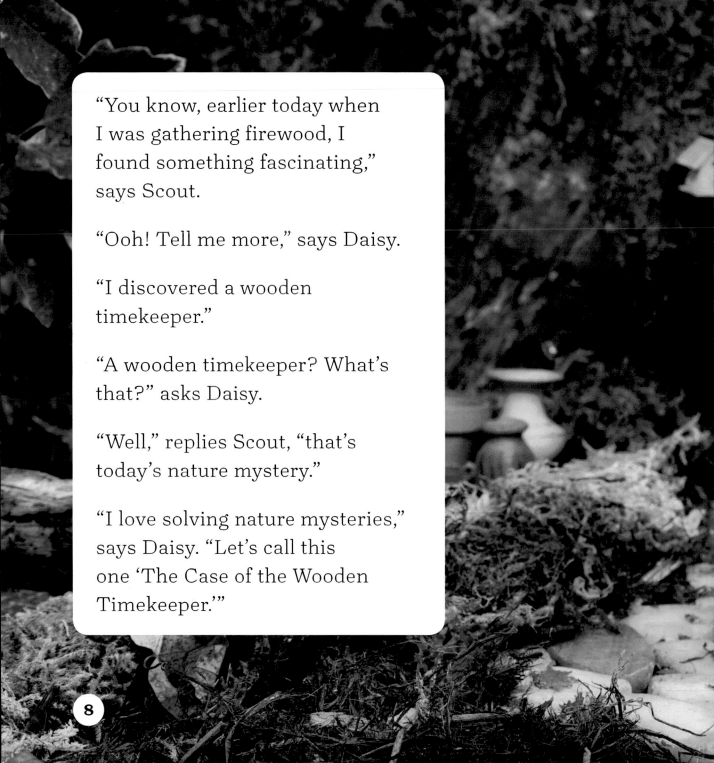

"You know, earlier today when I was gathering firewood, I found something fascinating," says Scout.

"Ooh! Tell me more," says Daisy.

"I discovered a wooden timekeeper."

"A wooden timekeeper? What's that?" asks Daisy.

"Well," replies Scout, "that's today's nature mystery."

"I love solving nature mysteries," says Daisy. "Let's call this one 'The Case of the Wooden Timekeeper.'"

Scout opens up his field notes.

"Have a look, Daisy. I sketched some clues that will help you solve the mystery," says Scout.

"Okay, let's go to the forest and look for more clues," suggests Daisy.

Forest

"There are a lot of beautiful trees in the forest," notes Daisy. "But where is the wooden timekeeper?"

"Here's another clue," says Scout, pointing to his field notes.

"A tree stump... oh! Look over there!" exclaims Daisy.

"That's the stump I found earlier," says Scout.

Tree Stump

"Here's the third clue," says Scout. "Rings."

"I don't see rings anywhere," says Daisy.

"Why don't you take a closer look at the stump?" suggests Scout.

Daisy leans in with her magnifying glass. "Oh! The rings are in the wood!" exclaims Daisy. "They go around the inside of this tree stump."

Rings

"How many?" asks Scout.

Daisy counts the rings: "1-2-3-4-5-6-7-8-9-10-11."

"Terrific!" says Scout. "Let's put the three clues together to solve The Case of the Wooden Timekeeper."

"We found the forest, a tree stump and some tree rings," lists Daisy. "So what's with the wooden timekeeper?"

"To the library!" says Scout.

At the library, Scout pulls a book from the shelf. Daisy reads aloud:

Many trees add a new layer of wood under their bark every year. This layer will start out light in color and become darker as the growing season comes to an end. This means you can count each dark ring as one year.

ANNUAL GROWTH RINGS OF A DOUGLAS FIR

① A seedling pokes up from the earth.

② The tree grows quickly, as shown by the widely spaced rings.

③ The tree is damaged by falling timber, as shown by the uneven rings.

④ The rings show strong, healthy years of steady growth.

⑤ The tree is burned by fire, as shown by the fire scar.

⑥ The narrow rings show years of slow growth.

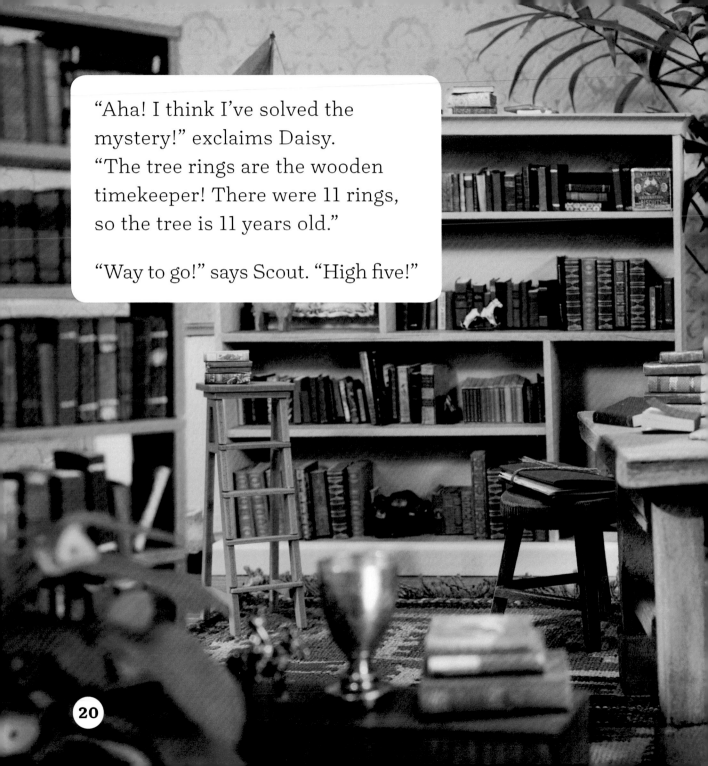

"Aha! I think I've solved the mystery!" exclaims Daisy. "The tree rings are the wooden timekeeper! There were 11 rings, so the tree is 11 years old."

"Way to go!" says Scout. "High five!"

Back in the forest, Scout and Daisy have a mindful moment.

"Trees are an important part of our ecosystem," says Scout. "They help keep our air clean by absorbing carbon dioxide and releasing oxygen — what we need in order to breathe."

"Let's pretend to be like a tree, Scout," suggests Daisy. "Plant one foot on the ground, and bend your other knee like I'm doing. Try to balance and stand tall like a tree. Lift your arms up in the air like branches. Now take a big, deep breath of fresh air."

"I've had such a fun time solving The Case of the Wooden Timekeeper," comments Daisy.

"Thanks for the great day!" says Scout. "Speaking of time, it's getting late. I'll walk you home."

"Thanks, Scout," says Daisy.

Later that evening, Scout is resting by the fire.

"What a day! I stacked firewood, helped Daisy solve a nature mystery and now..."

Scout yawns.

"...I think it's about *time* I go to bed. Goodnight, Gumboot Kids!"

Field Notes

Needles: Coniferous trees have needle-shaped leaves, which retain water and help the tree survive cold weather.

Branches: The part of a tree that grows out of its trunk with leaves, needles, flowers or fruit growing on it.

Trunk: The main, wide central stem of the tree. The branches grow from the trunk. The tree rings are found inside the trunk.

Roots: Roots anchor the tree to the ground and draw water and nutrients from the soil.

Needles

Branches

Trunk

Roots

Douglas Fir Tree

Most coniferous trees have needles instead of broad, flat leaves. They are often called evergreens because they stay green year-round.

Almost all deciduous trees drop their leaves in the fall, are dormant during the winter then produce new leaves when the weather warms up.

Coniferous trees produce cones. Some of the most well-known conifers are cedars, cypresses, firs, redwoods, pines and yews. Each of the tallest, heaviest and oldest living things on Earth are conifers.

Trees can live for hundreds, even thousands, of years. The oldest tree ever discovered is a Great Basin bristlecone pine with more than 5,000 rings!

A coast redwood in California is said to be the world's tallest tree at 115.56 m (379.1 ft).

Nature Craft

Inspired by a pinecone that fell from a tree, Daisy has crafted a mini Scout. Would you like to make a pinecone friend?

STEP 1

Head outside and collect some cones. Try looking under a coniferous tree, like a fir, spruce or pine.

STEP 2

Gather your craft supplies. You'll need glue, googly eyes, buttons, pipe cleaners, paper and paint. You can use craft glue or ask an adult to help you with a glue gun.

STEP 3

Use your imagination! Maybe your pinecone friend will have feet, wings, antennae or a tail. It's up to you. Have fun! And remember there's no right or wrong way to make a nature craft!

TELEVISION SERIES CREDITS

Created by Eric Hogan and Tara Hungerford
Produced by Tracey Mack
Developed for television with Cathy Moss
Music by Jessie Farrell

Television Consultants

Mindfulness: Molly Stewart Lawlor, Ph.D
Zoology: Michelle Tseng, Ph.D
Botany: Loren Rieseberg, Ph.D

BOOK CREDITS

Based on scripts for television by Tara Hungerford,
Cathy Moss and Eric Hogan
Production Design: Eric Hogan and Tara Hungerford
Head of Production: Tracey Mack
Character Animation: Deanna Partridge-David
Graphic Design: Rio Trenaman, Gurjant Singh
Sekhon and Lucas Green
Photography: Sean Cox
Illustration: Kate Jeong

Special thanks to the Gumboot Kids cast and crew,
CBC Kids, Shaw Rocket Fund, Independent Media
Fund, The Bell Fund, Canada Media Fund, Creative
BC, Playology, and our friends and family.

ADDITIONAL PHOTO CREDITS

30 Anick Violette (pinecone friends)

Shutterstock.com
30 Mike Braune (top pine cone), Chones (bottom
pine cone), Megapixels (glue), Kansitang Pittayanon
(craft supplies)

More GUMBOOT KIDS Nature Mysteries

Visit Scout and Daisy
gumbootkids.com

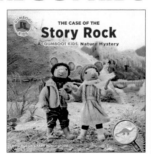